'Oh boy!' said Rat. 'What a mansion. I wonder whose it is?'

Uncle Charlie Weasel simply gaped. He was a weasel of the world, he had wintered in old boots, hollow trees, old car seats and rusty kettles – and he knew that here at last was the perfect place to live, both marvellous and strange.

'Folks,' he said at last, 'you are looking at Uncle Charlie Weasel's Winter Palace!'

SAM McBRATNEY

Uncle Charlie Weasel's Winter

Illustrated by Mike Daley

A Magnet Book

First published in 1988
by Methuen Children's Books Ltd
This Magnet paperback edition first published 1989
by Methuen Children's Books
A Division of OPG Services Ltd
Michelin House, 81 Fulham Road, London SW3 6RB
Text copyright © 1988 Sam McBratney
Illustrations copyright © 1988 Mike Daley

Printed in Great Britain by
Cox & Wyman Ltd, Reading

ISBN 0 416 13162 X

Contents

I
Winter
in a Welly Boot

Rat popped up his head from one of the bins at the edge of the woods. He looked rather wet and slimy, and he had a soggy lump of bread in one hand.

'I got one, Charlie,' he said, giddy with success, 'it's a bit damp and it doesn't half pong but it's a big fat juicy one!'

So are you, thought Uncle Charlie Weasel, the greediest weasel in the whole wide world. From time to time, when he got really hungry, he ate whichever rat happened to be his best friend at the time.

He accepted the sandwich and opened it into halves. His mouth, as he picked out a long ribbon of green stuff, curled unpleasantly to one side.

'What is this? A squashed leaf?'

'It's lettuce, Charlie.'

'Lettuce? *Lettuce*?' Uncle Charlie Weasel bared the points of his yellow teeth. 'No, no, no. What we want is meat, Rat. Bring me corned beef. Find me ham. Chicken-paste will do at a pinch, but *lettuce* . . .' – he patted Rat's sticky whiskers – 'let us have no more of this lettuce, you silly-billy.'

'Okay, Charlie, whatever you say.'

Where there are trash cans and litter-bins at the edges of the wood, there you will find Uncle Charlie Weasel. As a rule, he did not dig in the trash cans for his own food – he preferred to leave that sort of work to his best friend, Rat.

After another search-and-dive operation, Rat surfaced with the remains of an old beef hamburger. With this and other morsels, Uncle Charile retired to his home in the woods.

'Home' was a half-buried wellington boot. As he lay with his head poking out from his front door, Uncle Charlie Weasel sucked on a sausage and reflected that time was marching on. Summer had gone, Autumn was half over. Already the chestnut trees were dropping their heavy big leaves here, there and everywhere. Very soon, by Jove, the whole place would be stiff with frost.

Uncle Charlie took a long drink of crab-apple wine and sat up straight.

'I've just thought of something, Rat. Where am I going to sleep this winter? Eh?'

'In your welly boot, Charlie.'

'Are you kidding? That's where I spent last winter. It was so cold my tail froze stiff. Every time I turned over in my welly boot I thought it was going to snap off like a blasted icicle. And there's nothing to eat. And the trash cans are empty and everybody's asleep. What am I going to do?'

He jumped up and began to tramp through the fallen leaves in a terrible state.

'I'll starve. I will, you know. Last year my crab-apple wine froze in the jar, this year it'll be the blood in my lovely veins. I'll be a skeleton when I wake up, I won't know myself. Oh boy!'

Rat was amazed.

'But Charlie, haven't you put something aside for the winter? Everybody does – Hog, Foxy, Badger – we all do it. It's good standard practice to hoard some food.'

Uncle Charlie Weasel swallowed another draught of crab-apple wine, and slowly began to smile. A perfect idea had just come into his head.

'Don't talk to me about good standard practice, Rat. I know what I'll do, no need to panic. I'll go stay with my nephew on Crack Willow Hill.'

His nephew, Mr Stoat, lived in a cute little warm house that was lined with soft mosses and the down of feathery creatures. More to the point, the grub was super. In the mornings, the smell of grilled newts-on-toast wafted through all the rooms. Mrs Stoat's golden, crispy pies with their golden, crispy crusts were unforgettable works of art.

'But Charlie,' said Rat, 'you told me they didn't like you.'

'Of course they like me, I'm their Uncle. *She* doesn't like me, that Mrs Stoat, my nephew's blasted wife. She said I was a bad influence on her precious Little Ones, Harvey and Wilhemina. I'll tell you something, Rat – she threw me out last spring for no reason at all!'

That wasn't quite true. Mrs Stoat had put him out of the house because he gave Harvey and Wilhemina crab-apple wine, and because he called her friends names. Mrs Stoat did *not* like her very good friends Hog and Badger to be referred to as 'Stickleback' and 'Flatfeet'.

Yes, thought Uncle Charlie, Mrs Stoat could certainly be a problem. . . . Then he let out a yelp of delight.

'But of course! I've cracked it, Rat. Fetch me a stick, I want to make a crutch.'

Much puzzled, Rat ran off to oblige, and shortly returned with a suitable stick. Uncle Charlie Weasel padded the end that fitted under his armpit, then began to practise walking with a limp.

Perhaps, thought Rat, he's had too much crab-apple wine.

'Is your leg sore, Charlie?'

'More than sore. Almost broken, Rat!' He

staggered through the leaves, trailing his right leg and screwing up his face in agony. Eventually he came to rest against a tree.

'Now then. Suppose I came to your house like this, Rat. Would you not feel sorry for me? Would your heart not bleed? Could you send me away from your door? Eh?'

At last Rat saw the plan, and nodded wisely.

'Very clever, Charlie. Good. Very good.'

'Take my advice, Rat – if you want to get ahead, get a crutch. Let's go!'

Uncle Charlie Weasel set off for Crack Willow Hill with his crutch over one shoulder and a jar of wine over the other. Sometimes he paused to scan the trees for signs of Olly Owl. For the most part, though, he sang a merry little song, making up the words as he went along:

> 'Rat-a-tat-tat,
> Tootle your flute,
> Take it from me, it's by no means a hoot,
> To sleep for three months
> Stuck up a blasted welly boot. . . .'

2
The Mouse House
in the Woods

As Uncle Charlie Weasel set off for Crack
Willow Hill, something interesting was
happening just around a corner from the
trash cans. A blue van pulled off the road and
drove up a narrow track into the forest. One
of the five men who got out of the van opened
wide the back doors and, with a chorus of
grunts and sighs, they took hold of a large
wooden object and lowered it to the ground.

Many years had gone by since this object
was a beautiful piece of furniture in the
living-room of a fine, big house in the city.
Now, with its polished surface scratched like
a miniature ice rink, it was no longer wanted.
After taking up space in someone's garage for
several years, it was neglected and beyond
repair, and the men were dumping the done
old thing in the woods.

First, though, they made sure that no one was looking, for it was against the law to litter the countryside with town rubbish – then they staggered into the woods with their load until they came to a quiet clearing.

'Right, this'll do,' said one. 'Let 'er down. We should have got rid of it years ago.'

Their burden hit the ground with a bump. When the men walked away they left it standing in a tangle of ivy and bracken and ferns in the middle of a circle of beech trees. And only now did the mice inside begin to stir.

Every one of those mice had been holding on for dear life for at least half an hour – the journey had been unforgettable. Their furniture had taken to flying about the rooms and had dashed itself to pieces. The larder was bare. Crumbs of hard cheese and strips of crispy bacon littered the floor. The place was a mess, the house was a wreck and life, at that moment, seemed very tough indeed.

'At least we've stopped moving,' whispered one. His name was Claude. 'Where are we now, does anyone know? Who is going outside to have a look?'

Henry Streetmouse dusted himself down and listened with his large ears. It's mighty quiet out there, he thought.

'I'll go. When you hear three raps on the roof, you'll know it's all clear. And straighten those pictures on the walls, will you? Man, I hate crooked pictures on the walls.'

Away he went through the front door and up to the roof, from where he had a fine view of the surrounding territory – their new neighbourhood. He blinked his eyes twice, and then looked again. What he saw was incredible.

Henry Streetmouse and his company of Streetmice were used to screeching motor-cars, spitting cats, growling dogs, tramping feet and big-city bustle and buzz. Here, there was only silence. And the plants seemed to grow up to the sky! This was quite a sight for a mouse who was used to nothing much bigger than dandelions. Henry Streetmouse rapped the roof and summoned up the others.

Twenty-eight mice stood on their roof in a state of shock.

'Man, this is real weird,' said Mac.

'Where is everybody?' wondered Roscoff.

'This is some crummy joint,' observed Short Mouse.

'Maybe so,' said Henry Streetmouse, 'but we're here, mate. This is Home Sweet Home for us now and we just have to make the best of it. Let's go down and straighten some pictures.'

3
A Knock on
Mr Stoat's Door

Autumn had arrived on Crack Willow Hill. Oaks and beeches, great and small, let loose flurries of leaves on the squirrels below who were seeking nuts for their winter stores.

Young Wilhemina Stoat and her brother Harvey played hide-and-seek in the up-turned roots of the huge willow tree, while Mr Stoat, Badger, Buck Rabbit and Hog sat on the horizontal trunk of the tree. They were discussing the weather.

'Winter is a bother and a nuisance, you know, Stoaty,' said Hog, who was nursing an armful of dry leaves to line his den, 'and they're getting longer, winters are.'

'No they're not,' said Buck Rabbit.

'Personally speaking,' said Badger loudly, 'I have made thirteen black puddings to see me through until the spring.'

'Very wise,' Hog declared, 'I didn't waken up until April this year. Something has definitely gone wrong with our weather and I don't care what anyone says. What do you think, Stoaty?'

Mr Stoat was one of those folk who try to please everyone and who never have arguments.

'I think it will most likely be a short winter or a long one,' he said. 'Come along, Young Stoats, we must be off home or your mama will wonder what has happened to us – and to the pail of water we were supposed to bring back with us!'

Harvey and Wilhemina carried the pail of water down Foxy's Lane and into the broad Avenue where their house was. A wonderful smell of simmering stew met their noses as they climbed the steps.

'Mmmmm,' murmured Mr Stoat. He hung up his cap, placed his cane behind the door and immediately began to set the table. 'We are home, my Jewel,' he called out. 'Badger seems to feel that it may be a very cold winter. He has made thirteen black puddings to see him through.'

Mrs Stoat appeared with a steaming pot and approached the table.

'I have been thinking,' she said. 'What are you going to say to that creature when he shows up at our door and says that he wants to stay with us for the winter?'

By 'that creature' Mrs Stoat meant none other than Uncle Charlie Weasel. Mr Stoat was a little embarrassed.

'Well . . . he *is* family, my Dearest.'

'We like Uncle Charlie, Mama,' said Wilhemina. 'Don't we, Harvey?'

'I like Uncle Charlie,' said Harvey, 'he's funny.'

'Your Uncle Charlie is not a nice weasel, children. He tells lies. He hangs around trash cans all day and drinks that disgusting crab-apple wine. That filthy cap he wears never leaves his head. The last time he stayed with us he came home drunk and almost set the house on fire. This time you must be firm, Mr Stoat – and tell him No!'

'I shall indeed, I shall certainly be firm,' promised Mr Stoat, then cleverly changed the subject. 'I must say to you, my Jewel, that this stew is just the best thing for the time of year, and it is much appreciated by all of us. What is in it?'

'Mushroom and shrew.'

'Ah! Wonderful.'

The thick brown stew was ladled on to four dishes. A little was left in the pot. As Mrs Stoat often said, there were other days. She had just scolded Harvey for blowing on a hot spoonful when a knock happened at the door.

'Who can that be?' asked Wilhemina.

'Oh, I daresay it's our friend Hog,' said Mr Stoat, pushing back his seat. 'Wants to borrow some salt, I've no doubt.'

Mrs Stoat had stiffened in her chair. She knew that knock, and it wasn't Hog. When the door opened Uncle Charlie Weasel walked in.

Actually, he limped in on a crutch. Apparently he could hardly walk. His brown eyes rolled sadly as he looked about him, sniffing, and he said, 'Well, I just happened to be passing, Nephew. Thought I'd look you up and see how the Little Ones were getting on.'

'What happened to your poor leg, Uncle Charlie?' asked Wilhemina.

'Is it very sore?' asked Harvey.

'Well yes, it is,' said Uncle Charlie. 'It happened last week. I was coming to visit you when I noticed a very fine nest high up a tree and I said to myself, Uncle Charlie – you must get some eggs for Harvey and Wilhemina, those Little Ones love nothing better than some jolly fine birds' eggs. But I slipped, and I fell, and. . . . Well, hopefully, nothing is actually broken. And here I am. What's that smell?'

'Stew, Uncle Charlie,' said Wilhemina.

'Mushroom and shrew,' said Harvey.

Stew. Mushroom and shrew. The words fell on Uncle Charlie Weasel's ears like a beautiful line of poetry. Wincing with pain, he turned to face Mr Stoat.

'Nephew, I've been wondering. Seeing how I've got a bad leg and so forth . . . could

I stay here for a few days? Just until I get my strength back, of course, that goes without saying. It's a hard world out there for a one-legged weasel.'

Mr Stoat glanced nervously at his wife, who calmly laid down her spoon. 'Children, wait in the next room with your Uncle Charlie Weasel, I want to speak to your Papa.'

The room, when they had gone, was filled with a rather heavy silence.

'Perhaps he has changed, my dear,' said Mr Stoat uneasily.

'He is Uncle Charlie Weasel, Mr Stoat – he cannot change. Even his knock has remained the same. He has no manners and he spreads germs. Besides, he is a bad influence on our Young Stoats. You know very well that he is everything we would wish them not to be.'

'Yes. Well, yes. I would normally agree with you, my Precious, but he is our Uncle. It is not a good example to send away one of our own relations who may have a badly broken leg.'

A row in the Stoat household was almost unknown. Sometimes Mr Stoat gave way, sometimes not. On this occasion, Mrs Stoat backed down. She opened the door and called the others in to hear the verdict.

'You may stay with us, Uncle Charlie Weasel, under certain conditions. You will tidy your room. You will wash. You will not wear your cap in the house and you will not drink crab-apple wine.'

Snob, thought Uncle Charlie Weasel. Out loud, he said: 'Absolutely not!' and walked to the door of the spare bedroom, yawning. 'I think I'll lie down and take the weight off my leg. I was just wondering . . . what time is breakfast at in the morning?'

'When it's ready,' said Mrs Stoat.

'I see. May I inquire what is on the . . . eh . . . the menu?'

'Badger has kindly sent us a black pudding. We shall eat some of it for breakfast.'

'Ah. Well, goodnight, my Little Ones, and sleep well.'

He limped into the bedroom, thinking how he couldn't care less whether they slept well or dreamed all night long about Olly Owl. Before getting into bed he hung his crutch on the back of the door, put on his cap, then carefully transferred his secret jar of crab-apple wine from under his jacket to under the bed. Only now did he lie down and close his eyes with a sigh.

Black pudding, he was thinking. Mmmmm. What a way to start the day!

4
Danger
in the Trees

Four mice talked quietly in the moonlight about old times.

'You know what I miss most?' Roscoff said dreamily. 'I miss drainpipes. I used to love climbing up drainpipes.'

'Me too,' said Mac.

The Short Mouse sighed. He was recalling the taste of crispy bacon.

'Cheese,' said Claude. 'I'd give my whiskers for a big lump of cheese. I bet we never get to eat cheese again.'

A hush came over the conversation as each brought to mind the good things about living in the big city. They were four very fine mice. Roscoff wore a fetching blue and golden bandana at his throat; Mac carried at his side a sword that was as sharp as a needle (in fact it was a needle); Claude's

magnificent white whiskers seemed to glow
in the light of the moon; and the Short
Mouse was no shorter than any of the others
– until you looked at his tail and realised
that it wasn't there. A ship's cook on a
Portsmouth ferry had one day removed it
with a carving knife and the tail had ended
up in the crew's stew.

They were joined by their leader, Henry
Streetmouse. Henry himself was inclined to
be a dandy, as anyone could easily observe
from the bold colours of his hat and the
round rings in his large ears. In his walk
there was a suggestion of a swagger, as if he

had been aware from an early age that he had been born to be something of a boss.

'Everybody's hungry,' he said. 'We're off to get something to eat.'

Twenty-eight mice marched into the woods to find food. This was no easy matter in the dark, for they tripped over one another at regular intervals.

'We could do with a few streetlamps round here,' grumbled Mac.

Presently they came to an open glade where some late-flowering dandelions grew among patches of wild grass. The seed-heads on the grass were so heavy and ripe that they almost trailed on the ground. Grass seed was not crispy bacon nor cheese, but it was food of a sort. Twenty-seven hungry mice got ready to charge.

'Wait a minute,' said Henry Streetmouse suspiciously. 'There's something not right about this place. I don't like it.'

He didn't like the way the moon shone down exactly where the grass grew, like a spotlight. He didn't like the dark hollows, like caves, in the enormous tree above. And why hadn't that fine crop of seed been gobbled up by someone else?

'Henry,' said Mac, 'we're hungry, mate. Let's eat.'

'All right. Move in, everybody, and fill your pockets. And don't hang about.'

The mice worked busily in pairs – one bent over a blade of grass, the other stripped off the seeds. None of them heard the faint flutter of wings in the tree above as Olly Owl left his branch. He was the deadliest night-hunter in the woods.

A flicker in the corner of his eye made Henry Streetmouse glance up. And he saw – somewhere between himself and the silver moon – a moving black shadow. He had never seen the like of it before. It was as if a flying cat was simply dropping out of the sky.

'Beat it!' he yelled to Claude, his partner. 'Everybody get out of here – fast!' Then the shadow landed, covered him, thrashed him into the ground, seemed to bury him.

Olly Owl rose into the air with something in his talons. Henry Streetmouse shook himself, and blinked. Mac was beside him.

'You okay, Henry?'

'I think so. Just dazed. Man, did you see it? What was that thing?'

'I don't know. I have to tell you, Henry – it got Claude. There are only twenty-seven of us, now.'

What a miserable thing to happen, thought Henry Streetmouse. Poor old Claude, one of his oldest and best friends, had been right about thing – he never got to taste cheese again.

Henry Streetmouse drew his sword and shook it at the tree above.

'Wait till the next time, Buster,' he called. 'We'll be ready for you.'

5
Uncle Charlie Weasel Does Something Bad

Uncle Charlie Weasel washed every day. He did not come to the breakfast table in his cap and braces. He didn't 'talk rough', as Mrs Stoat called it, and he never drank crab-apple wine during the hours of daylight. He was on his very best behaviour, of course, because the last thing he wanted was to spend the winter curled up in a cold welly boot.

But he longed to do something bad! He longed to shout 'Flatfeet!' at silly old Badger and then run away, or play an all-night game of cards with Johnny the Ferret. Oh, how he longed to perch on the rim of a trash can and sniff and sniff and sniff!

He couldn't do any of these things. Mrs Stoat would put him out. One day she set a bucket in his hand and said, 'Take that to the river, Uncle Charlie, and fill it for me please.'

'What about my sore leg?' said Uncle Charlie, raising up his crutch.

'What about it? Take the Young Stoats with you, they will help.'

'Oh please yes, Uncle Charlie,' cried Harvey and Wilhemina, 'we'll go with you.'

Spoilt little brats, thought Uncle Charlie Weasel. But he smiled pleasantly and said that of course they could come.

Off they went. Uncle Charlie Weasel led the way up the Avenue, under Crack Willow and into the gloom of the forest. For someone with a bad leg he could certainly limp very fast, thought Wilhemina, who soon began to get worried.

'Are you sure this is the way to the river, Uncle Charlie?'

'All roads lead to rivers, Sweety Pie,' came the reply. 'I'm looking for a tree marked with an X. I'm sure it's round here somewhere . . . ah!'

The tree marked with an X had a hollow trunk. Inside the trunk was a hidden jar of crab-apple wine. Uncle Charlie Weasel took a long swig, wiped his mouth, and made himself comfortable on a pile of dry leaves.

'Aaaaaah! Yes indeed! Life is what you make it, Young Stoats. Trust your Uncle Charlie, he knows best. Life can be fun. Sometimes.'

He sniffed, and stared straight ahead. 'I have just seen the tail of a squirrel disappear into the trunk of that tree. Unless I am very much mistaken, its arms were full of goodies. Tell me, my Little Ones – are you hungry? Do you like nuts?'

Harvey and Wilhemina nodded. They were always hungry. Uncle Charlie Weasel limped to the tree and tapped it with his crutch.

A squirrel poked out her head.

'Pardon me, my Good Lady,' said Uncle Charlie Weasel, 'but are you aware that a fire has broken out?'

'A fire? What sort of fire?'

'The sort that burns, Madam – a forest fire. It is leaping from branch to branch, consuming tree after tree. Even as we speak the wind is driving it closer with every passing second.'

'That is terrible news,' said the squirrel, 'I must tell the others.' And she dashed away, looking serious.

Immediately Uncle Charlie Weasel's whippy tail disappeared into the squirrel

house. Harvey followed him in, then Wilhemina, wide-eyed and anxious. She wasn't sure that Mama would approve of this.

A cupboard door creaked as Uncle Charlie Weasel opened it. 'Aha! Tut-tut-tut-tut, but me no buts, such a lot of nuts. Who knows where the goodies are?' And he swept the contents of an entire shelf into his cap. 'Now follow me, Young Stoats, to where we can have a pleasant little snack between meals.'

They sat down under an oak tree, where Uncle Charlie Weasel tipped out the contents of his cap, and examined them.

'What have we here? Let's see . . . some catkins, nuts, haws, mushrooms. . . . Disappointing, really. Squirrels will eat anything but meat, the blasted vegetarians. There's not even a hairy caterpillar here!'

'Uncle Charlie,' said Wilhemina, 'there wasn't a fire.'

'True, very true.'

'Then you told lies. Mama doesn't allow us to tell lies.'

'Dear innocent child. Look at this acorn. The oak tree who grew it didn't grow it just for the squirrels. Acorns belong to everybody. Trust your Uncle Charlie Weasel, kids – eat up and be happy.'

On the way back to Crack Willow Hill, Uncle Charlie told Harvey and Wilhemina about the trash cans. He said you could lick the insides of many tins and taste mushy peas and sticky, sweet apricot juice. It sounded wonderful.

'Tomorrow,' he said, 'I shall take you to the trash cans.'

'Oh goody,' said Harvey.

'But do not mention to your mama that we're going, or where we've been today. She doesn't understand these things. Promise?'

'I promise!' said Harvey.

'I suppose so,' said Wilhemina.

Wilhemina was worried. That night she had a short talk with Harvey before they fell asleep.

'Harvey?'

'What?'

'Really, we stole that squirrel's food.'

'No we didn't, Uncle Charlie Weasel says acorns belong to everybody.'

'Should we go to the trash cans tomorrow?'

'Yes,' said Harvey. 'I want to lick some tins.' Then he fell asleep.

6
Excitement
at the Trash Cans

Uncle Charlie Weasel sang a song as he rushed through the woods on his crutch.

> *'Yippee!*
> *Oh the trash cans, the trash cans,*
> *That's where I like to be.*
> *There's baked beans and sardines,*
> *Yummy yummy yummeee!'*

And he added, with a shout, 'Shake a leg there, Young Stoats, we haven't got all day.'

Harvey and Wilhemina struggled to keep up with him. 'I don't see how he can go so fast with a sore leg,' grumbled Harvey.

Wilhemina was still worried. They were a long way from home in a strange part of the forest, and Mama didn't know they were here. She would have a fit!

But the trash cans, when they arrived,

were brimming gloriously with heaps upon heaps of rubbish. Every little breeze that passed was filled with smells both sweet and sour. A flock of peaceful crows rose up in alarm as Uncle Charlie Weasel raced at them, brandishing his crutch like a weapon.

'Get off my property, you greedy brutes!' Harvey and Wilhemina were too full of the wonders of the place to notice that he wasn't limping any more.

Suddenly, something awful popped out of a bin. Harvey clung to Wilhemina nervously, for he had never seen anything like it. The creature's fur was wet, as if it had come into contact with all kinds of dribbles, juices and squelches, and an empty carton was lodged on its head at a jaunty angle.

'Ah, Rat,' said Uncle Charlie Weasel, 'say Hello to my nephew's Little Ones.'

'Hello,' said Rat obediently.

'How do you do,' said Wilhemina.

'Pleased to meet you,' said Harvey, though he wasn't actually sure whether he was pleased or not. He was certain that Mama would never approve of such a rough creature.

'Okay, Rat, find them something nice to eat. This is their first time at the trash cans, so make it something special.'

'I'll try, Charlie. I'll go right to the bottom.'

Rat upended himself, and disappeared for such a long time that Wilhemina was sure he must have suffocated down there.

Not a bit of it. Presently Rat rose out of the rubbish, and his eyes were shining with triumph.

'Sunken treasure, Charlie! I got three chicken bones.'

'Well done, good friend, well done indeed. Now get us something to drink, if you please.'

They began to eat. After the chicken bones they feasted on grains of rice and some lumps of fatty beef. Wilhemina licked some wrappers until they had no taste left, and Harvey drained the last dribbles out of many cans. Finally they finished off some fish in soggy brown batter, and lay down to rest.

'Uncle Charlie, we should go home now,' said Wilhemina. 'The sun is turning red.'

'Mama might be worried about us,' said Harvey.

Let her worry, thought Uncle Charlie Weasel. But he said, 'Very well. The day is done, we've had our fun. Let's go, I know a short-cut.' Snatching up his crutch, he set off at an alarming rate down a dark tunnel of thicket and thorn, which brought them eventually into a patch of dappled light. Here, they set eyes on one of the most extraordinary objects ever seen.

Its four legs were sunk in tufts of coarse grass, as if the thing had somehow taken root there, and grown. These legs supported a large, odd-shaped box, with a flat roof; and the box, besides, was made of dark and polished wood.

'Oh boy!' Rat was overawed. 'What a mansion. I wonder whose it is?'

Uncle Charlie Weasel simply gaped. He was a weasel of the world, he had wintered in old boots, hollow trees, old car seats and rusty kettles – and he knew that here at last was the perfect place to live, both marvellous and strange.

'Folks,' he said at last, 'you are looking at Uncle Charlie Weasel's Winter Palace!'

7
Uncle Charlie Weasel's Winter Palace

'Do you think anybody acutally lives in it?' asked Rat. 'I mean, it might belong to Foxy. What'll you do then, Charlie?'

Good thinking, thought Uncle Charlie Weasel. Foxes were far too big to mess about with. He threw a friendly arm around Rat's shoulder.

'Go up and rap on the door, Rat, there's a good fellow.'

'But, Charlie. . . .'

'I shall be right here, ready to protect you. Go on, now, don't be a silly Rat.' And he tapped Rat rather firmly with his crutch.

Poor Rat bristled with nerves as he crept forward, watched by Uncle Charlie Weasel and by Harvey and Wilhemina. Timidly he rapped on a carved wooden leg and said, 'Excuse me, please, is anyone in? Who lives there, please?'

*

Inside their mouse house, Henry Streetmouse and his Streetmouse friends were preparing to hop into bed.

Twenty-eight hammocks hung from the various nuts and bolts that held their mouse house together. One of the hammocks was empty, of course, for they had not yet taken down Claude's in the hope that he might still come home.

Henry Streetmouse lay back and did some thinking as his hammock swung to and fro. It had been a good day. The mysterious flying cat had attacked them once again and they had been ready for it. Twenty-seven mice armed with long poles had sent it back to the trees with something to think about. Perhaps life in the forest was not so bad after all. . . .

There came a tapping noise outside. Twenty-seven hammocks swayed as the mice in them sat up.

Could that possibly be Claude? Henry Streetmouse dashed to the front door and saw a rat on the ground. It was hitting the leg of the house with a long stick.

'Beat it, Buster!' said Henry Streetmouse. 'You're on our patch. This is private property.

You are trespassing. So buzz-buzz. Get on your bike and zoomy-zoom-zoom.'

While the rat stared at Henry Streetmouse in blank amazement, another creature, altogether different, walked forward and announced himself.

'The name is Uncle Charlie Weasel, mouse. You got two minutes to get out of my house, then I'm coming in. One, two, and counting. . . .'

Henry did not like the look of that weasel character. There was a nasty big stick in his hand, a mean gleam in his eye.

'This is not your house, we live here. I warn you we shall fight, we shall never surrender. There are twenty-seven of us.'

'If I get the hold of *you*, mousy-wousy, there'll only be twenty-six. CHAAARGE!'

Up went the crutch. With a hair-raising yell, and all his teeth showing, Uncle Charlie Weasel raced at the mouse house and jumped on the roof. Once there, he began to beat on it joyfully with his crutch, as if he'd found a wonderful big drum.

Inside, the noise was deafening. Mac folded his ears in two.

'Who *is* that out there?'

'Think of the meanest cat you ever saw,'

said Henry Streetmouse. 'Well, he's worse. He's wild. What are we going to do?'

Panic broke out. If Henry Streetmouse did not know what to do, what hope could there be? An upside-down face appeared at the front door, and spoke.

'Out you come, mousy-wousies. Out of the housy-wousy like good little mousy-wousies.'

The Short Mouse grabbed a pole, as if to poke the intruder in the eye with it, but Henry stopped him.

'No. Do as he says, pack up your belongings.'

Roscoff was aghast.

'You mean . . . give up our house?'

'We can't beat him – not right now. We should have been ready for this, and we weren't. If we go now, we can live to fight another day.'

Sadly, twenty-seven mice began to take down their hammocks.

Harvey and Wilhemina, who were watching these events outside, were amazed to see how well Uncle Charlie Weasel could run. There was obviously nothing wrong with his leg, for he was dancing madly on the roof of the strange house.

'He hasn't got a sore leg at all,' said Harvey.

'He was only fooling us,' said Wilhemina. 'Look, here they come.'

One by one, the mice appeared at the door and slid to the ground. Each carried a bundle of belongings in a backpack and they looked really miserable. I wouldn't like to be put out of my house, thought Wilhemina.

'Uncle Charlie, I don't think that's fair,' she said. 'Those mice were there first and now you've put them out.'

'Where will they go?' asked Harvey.

'Who cares?' said Uncle Charlie Weasel. 'They're only blasted mice.'

A mouse with rings in his ears spoke up rather bravely. 'Wherever we go, we shall be back. You can count on it.' And with that, the long line of evicted mice marched off into the woods.

Uncle Charlie Weasel did not see them go – he was too busy squeezing through the front door of his exciting new home.

'Oh boy!' It was huge! 'Look at the height of that ceiling. What a place! You couldn't dream it up in your dreams, I shall stack it with lots of lovely, lovely grub for all those rainy rainy days, I shall lie like a King all winter . . .' – he stretched out his arms in delirium – '. . . Uncle Charlie Weasel's Winter Palace!'

Voices spoke outside.

'Uncle Charlie?'

'We want to go home.'

Those blasted Young Stoats. He'd forgotten all about them. He jumped to the ground.

'Home? I am home. *This* is home.'

'But we don't live here,' said Wilhemina, 'we want to go to out own house on Crack Willow Hill.'

Uncle Charlie Weasel pointed towards the forest with his crutch.

'Off you go, then – it's that way.'

'But we'll get lost.'

'And it's getting dark.'

'Tough,' said Uncle Charlie Weasel.

Harvey and Wilhemina Stoat looked at one another, then at the darkening sky, and walked into the forest on their own.

8
In the Dark Woods

From her window Mrs Stoat looked anxiously down The Avenue. It was dark outside. The stars were ominously bright and a pale moon hung over the quiet forest like a cold, unfriendly eye. And her Young Stoats had not yet come home.

'Mr Stoat?'

'Yes, my dearest?'

'When I get my hands on that Charlie Weasel he will need more than crutches by the time I have finished with him. Where *are* they? Where can they possibly be?'

Mr Stoat struggled into his best hunting-jacket – which was held for him by Hog – and slipped into a pair of stout boots. It had been raining outside, there would certainly be puddles.

He joined Mrs Stoat at the window. Several sunken moons shimmered in the puddles that had formed in The Avenue.

Olly Owl hooted twice. Seen between the showers and in such a light, Crack Willow Hill looked as pretty as a picture, but of course it was all very worrying. An owl like Olly would spot two small stoats with no bother at all.

Mr Stoat tried not to show his concern.

'I think we should look on the bright side of things. After all, we do not know the facts.'

'What facts!' Mrs Stoat said this so loudly that Hog gave a jump. 'Harvey and Wilhemina went for a walk this afternoon with their Uncle Charlie Weasel and they are not back yet. They should have been in bed two hours ago. What other facts do you need, Mr Stoat?' And she added grimly, 'I knew I should never have let them go.'

'Perhaps they are resting somewhere. Uncle Charlie Weasel's leg may be giving him pain.'

'Pain my foot!' Mrs Stoat threw on her cloak. 'I shall come with you.'

'No, no. Someone must stay here in case they return of their own accord. You must see that makes sense, my dearest. My friend Hog will be with me and he has excellent night-sight. This is very good of you, Hog.'

'Not a bit of it, Stoaty,' said Hog.

After a last look in the mirror – Mr Stoat liked to be properly dressed for all occasions, even dangerous ones – he left with these comforting words: 'I am confident that all will be well.'

Harvey and Wilhemina Stoat were lost.

They huddled up together at the mouth of a disused rabbit hole and listened to the forest dripping. There were loud drips close by and soft drips in the distance, like echoes. All that dripping made the forest feel like an enormous, empty place – as if there were somehow more trees by night than by day.

It wasn't empty, of course. Olly Owl was out there somewhere. Their mama and papa had always told them never to go near Olly Owl's tree because you couldn't hear him, you couldn't smell him and you couldn't see him – not until he had plucked you off the ground with those big pointy feet.

But there were so many trees.

'How are we supposed to know which one is Olly Owl's tree?' whispered Wilhemina.

'I don't know,' said Harvey.

'And how could Uncle Charlie Weasel be so mean to us? He didn't even have a sore leg, you know.'

'I know,' said Harvey.

They decided to move on. Eventually they came to an open space, where a patch of ripe grass rippled in a quiet little breeze. The seedheads of dandelions glowed eerily, like moonlamps.

'Harvey, do you fell as if eyes are watching us from everywhere?'

'Yes,' whispered Harvey.

'And do you hear things?'

Harvey nodded. He heard breaking twigs and falling leaves and drippy-drip-drip.

A passing cloud unveiled the moon. They looked up and saw the silvery outline of a puffed-up ball of feathers.

'Oh Harvey! He's up there on a branch. Don't look at him, just run!'

It was all very well for Wilhemina to shout, Run. But Harvey couldn't run. He was just too afraid to move a muscle – it was as if Olly Owl had the power to make him stay exactly where he was. Even when the great night hunter spread his wings and began to drop, Harvey remained where he was and could not move.

The falling shape darkened everything, and
he knew that Olly Owl was upon him.

I shall never see Mama and Papa again,
thought Harvey.

Then there came the sound of many voices
in the night – high little voices, squeaky with
excitement.

'Up and at 'im, Streetmice!'

'Wallop, bash and umph!'

'There's one up the eye for good old Claude. Hurray!'

More cheers broke out as Olly Owl let out a screech of astonishment. He was not used to being prodded and bashed in all kinds of delicate places by twenty-seven mouse poles. Up and away he flew, as fast as a pair of wings would carry him. And Harvey Stoat found himself looking at a funny little character with a pole over his shoulder. The mouse was wearing an extraordinary hat and rings in his large ears.

'Are you going to lie there all day, mate? We'd best get out of here before that flying pussy comes back.'

They brought Harvey into the shelter of a beech tree's arching roots. Naturally it was some time before Harvey recovered from his ordeal, and when he did, he had to face Wilhemina.

'I told you not to look at that brute, Harvey Stoat. If it hadn't been for Henry Streetmouse and his Streetmouse friends you would have been finished. You would have been owl's dinner. You would have been chewed up and swallowed in tiny little bits.'

She turned gratefully to the mouse in the hat. 'You are very, very brave, Henry Streetmouse. All of you are very brave.'

Henry Streetmouse did not deny it.

'We grew up in a tough neighbourhood. Man, you should see some of the pussies we came up against. Mind you, they couldn't fly like his nibs up there. Shhh!' he broke off, mouse pole at the ready. 'Somebody's coming.'

Some twigs snapped in the undergrowth; heavy panting was heard and a disgusted snort as a foot stepped in a puddle. Mr Stoat came into view with Hog in close attendance.

'It's Papa!' cried Wilhemina.

Harvey and Wilhemina greeted him with hugs. They did not attempt to hug Hog. Hugging a hedgehog is not much fun.

'Where have you been today, you silly Young Stoats!' declared Mr Stoat.

He never found it easy to be cross. All the same, Mr Stoat was clearly far from pleased as he stood there, his new boots glistening with mud.

'We must go home immediately, everybody is worried about you. On the way you will kindly explain, Young Stoats, why you have been away from home for such a long time!'

And he glanced, first, at Olly Owl's tree, then at the curious sight of twenty-seven mice standing in battle formation, mouse poles at the ready.

The door was already open when they got back home – Mrs Stoat had seen them coming down The Avenue. Of course she was delighted to see Harvey and Wilhemina safe and well, but she was absolutely amazed when all those mice tramped into her house in single file.

'I'm afraid there are twenty-seven of them, my jewel,' said Mr Stoat, scratching his head. Normally he loved to offer chairs to his guests. 'Allow me to introduce Mr Henry Streetmouse and his Streetmouse friends.'

Mrs Stoat listened to the story of Harvey's wonderful rescue from Olly Owl.

'So you see, my dear,' finished Mr Stoat, 'these poor fellows have nowhere to sleep tonight. I'm afraid I took the liberty of inviting them home without consulting you.'

Her reply came immediately.

'They can stay here, Mr Stoat. Charlie Weasel's room will be empty.'

'I knew you would be generous, my dear one!' Mr Stoat turned to Henry Streetmouse and began a long speech to thank him for saving the lives of his Little Ones. Mr Stoat loved making speeches. He said all the right things, and he said them very well.

9
Unhappy Hog

The folk who lived on Crack Willow Hill loved coversation. Even on a cold day in November, Buck Rabbit and Badger and Mr Stoat sat on the mossy trunk of the old tree to exchange ideas, opinions and gossip.

While the grown-ups talked, Harvey and Wilhemina Stoat played with Henry Streetmouse and his Streetmouse friends in Foxy's Lane. They were learning interesting new city games like 'Tickle the Cat' and 'Mouse, Mouse, Mouse, Bring Home the Cheese'.

Meanwhile, the conversation among the grown-ups turned to burglary.

'The squirrels are having a hard time of it, you know,' said Buck Rabbit thoughtfully. 'Somebody is breaking into their homes and stealing all their food. I mean, it's a very bad

business, what with winter just around the next corner.'

'Very bad,' muttered Badger. 'Talking of food, Stoaty, I think you must be running a hotel down there. How can you possibly accommodate all those mice?'

Mr Stoat sighed. It wasn't easy. Mrs Stoat had almost fainted when twenty-seven of the little chaps appeared for breakfast that morning.

'All the same, Badger,' he said, 'one must repay one's debts. Had it not been for them, my Harvey and Wilhemina would not be here today. In any case, Foxy has a spare den at the end of the lane, so perhaps he'll do me a favour.'

'Mind you,' continued Badger, 'I never was keen on that weasel chap who used to live with you. Dash it, the shifty fellow never seemed to look you in the eye, yet he always seemed to be watching you. How did he manage that?'

Hog interrupted the conversation. He was in such a hurry that he knocked over Wilhemina Stoat and didn't even pause to apologise.

'Something dreadful has happened,' he called out. 'Oh dear, I tell you frankly, things could not be much worse.'

It was very odd to see Hog so hot and bothered on such a cold morning. 'I woke up this morning and it was gone. All gone. You will have to come and see. All of you!'

As they hurried down The Avenue, Hog had a strange tale to relate. During the night, while he had been out helping Mr Stoat to search for Harvey and Wilhemina, someone had entered his house and made off with his food – every pick of it.

'And that's not all,' Hog finished dramatically, ushering his friends into the house. 'Look! They took my furniture as well. I haven't a stick of it left!'

The larder was empty, the room was bare. There wasn't even a chair for Hog to sit on, and he suddenly looked as though he needed to sit down.

'What can I do? Winter is coming, Stoaty, the first frost could be down on us any day. I am finished!'

'Look here, Hoggy,' said Badger, 'try not to be miserable. You can have one of my black puddings. No, by jove – you can have *two* black puddings.'

Buck Rabbit and Mr Stoat immediately offered to lend him some furniture. Poor Hog was quite overcome by their kindness and didn't have the heart to admit to Badger that he hated black pudding.

A thoughtful Buck Rabbit sucked noisily on his pipe. First the squirrels, he was thinking, and now Hog . . .

'You know, there's something very peculiar going on around here,' he stated soberly.

10
Rat Tries
to Sell a Brush

It was late in the afternoon. Dusk was already making everything vague as Uncle Charlie Weasel jogged through the forest with an empty sack over each shoulder. Struggling alongside on short, twinkling legs came Rat.

Rat carried a large case and he cast many a glance to the heavens above. It was a little early for Olly Owl to be out and about, but you never could tell with that feathered beast.

However, Olly Owl was not the main reason why Rat appeared to be very much on edge this evening. There was another reason, a huge reason. Poor Rat's tummy did somersaults every time he thought about it.

'Charlie, do you think this is really

necessary? Haven't you enough food now? Your b-big house is nearly full already.'

Rats are such wimps, thought Uncle Charlie Weasel. Stupid, too. There was no such thing as too much food, you could never get enough of it – especially black puddings.

'Don't be nervous, Rat,' he said. 'I hope you're going to be a good Rat and stick to our plan. You won't be a silly-billy, will you?'

'I'll not be a silly-billy, Charlie,' Rat said loyally.

All the same, his knees were knocking when they arrived soon afterwards under the elderberry bush opposite Badger's house.

They were going to burgle big Basher Badger! Was such a thing possible, wondered Rat? Trembling to the tips of his whiskers, he listened to the plan once again.

'Okay, this is how we do it. Basher has a front door and a back door. You rap the front door and sell him your brushes. I'll nip in the back door and fill the sacks with black puddings.'

'Charlie?'

'What?'

'Suppose he doesn't want to b-b-buy my brushes?'

'Of course he'll buy brushes, he's long and shaggy, isn't he? Anyway it doesn't matter, I'll be in and out again before old Flatfeet knows what's hit him. Carry on, Rat, there's a good chap – and keep him talking.'

As Rat crossed The Avenue he mumbled, 'Keep him talking, keep him talking . . .' He rapped on the door, stood well back, and almost fainted clean away.

Oh boy, this was a big Badger!

'Yes? What do you want?'

'Would you like to b-b-buy a b-b . . .'

'A *what*?' boomed Badger.

'Buy a b-b-badger b-b-b . . .'

'Would I like to buy a badger? What do you mean? I *am* a badger.'

'No,' said Rat, opening his case, 'I mean a b-b-brush.'

He mopped his brow. It wasn't going well. I'm not cut out for this sort of thing, thought Rat. 'My b-b-brushes are very cheap, if you'd like one,' he said.

'No. I wouldn't.'

'Oh.' Rat looked at the brush in his hand. 'Perhaps I could just give it to you for your long and shaggy coat.'

'I don't want a brush,' said Badger.

'You don't? Well . . . maybe you know another b-badger you could give it to?'

'Nope,' said Badger, folding his arms in the manner of one who is losing his patience.

Rat began to back away. 'In that case I'll just, eh . . . I'll just take it away with me, shall I? Yes.'

Rat did just that. He turned suddenly and bolted across The Avenue into the dark relief of the forest, where he kept on running. Soon he realised that someone was after him – someone who had longer legs than he had, someone who was catching him fast. He threw himself to the ground, ready to scream 'Surrender' when he saw that it was not Badger on his tail.

'Oh, Charlie! Charlie, I thought you were him. I thought I was done for.'

Uncle Charlie Weasel could not care less what Rat thought. He was ecstatic.

'Got them! What a haul. I got all of his black puddings. Boy, would I like to be a fly on the wall when Flatfeet opens his cupboard doors. Yoweee!'

At that very moment, as Uncle Charlie Weasel cried 'Yoweee!', Harvey and Wilhemina Stoat helped Mr Stoat to set table for the evening meal.

'Daddy,' said Wilhemina, 'Henry Streetmouse is teaching us how to play "Mouse, Mouse, Mouse Bring Home the Cheese".'

'And "Tickle the Cat",' said Harvey. 'He's our friend.'

'Jolly good,' Mr Stoat said. 'He sounds like a most interesting mouse.'

'Daddy, do you think Henry will be happy living in Foxy's old den?'

'Oh I should say so, my dote. It hasn't been lived in for a while and it may be rather damp, but they're tough characters, never fear.'

'Uncle Charlie Weasel stole their house. Henry says they're going to get it back.'

The door opened and Mrs Stoat entered with a steaming pie.

'Don't mention your Uncle Charlie Weasel in this house,' she said, placing the pie between a plate of grilled grubs and a dish full of peeled, boiled eggs, 'and don't you pair ever go to those trash cans again or you'll grow up to be just like him!'

She sank a knife into the pie, releasing a powerful, meaty odour. Just then they heard the beginnings of a great commotion outside. Mr Stoat dashed to the window.

'Seems like a rumpus of some kind. Badger is making a lot of fuss. I say, he's thrashing the trunk of the holly tree with a big stick!'

The Stoats, like everyone else who lived in and about The Avenue, rushed outside to see what the matter was. Foxy and Hog were already there, Buck Rabbit and one or two hares arrived at the same time as the Stoats. Squirrels gathered in the trees and even Mole stuck his head above ground to see Badger shaking his fists and roaring at the top of his voice.

'I've been robbed. They took my black

puddings, every last one, my lovely black puddings. What is the world coming to if a chap can't keep his black puddings? Heads are going to roll, Stoaty. Mark my words – *heads will roll*!'

Even the leaves in the trees seemed to tremble with sympathetic rage.

11
The Meeting
at Crack Willow

Uncle Charlie Weasel lay on the smooth top of his Winter Palace, basking in a pleasing glow of sunshine at high noon.

It was possibly the last sunshine of the year, but Uncle Charlie Weasel did not have a care in the world. Below him, in his house, he had more food then he could eat.

He sipped some crab-apple wine and spoke to his friend, Rat.

'Want to know something, Rat? This time last year I was getting ready to climb into a welly boot. Just look at me now! I got nuts, dried shrew, pickled newts, assorted grubs, black puddings, batches of snails, seeds . . .' He gave up trying to remember. 'Guess how many eggs I got stashed away.'

'Ten, Charlie.'

'Not even close, Rat – I got forty-eight. I

am a very important weasel. I am probably the wealthiest weasel in the world. Boy, am I some weasel!'

'But Charlie, what'll you do if they suspect you of stealing all their food?'

A crafty smile crossed Uncle Charlie Weasel's face. He'd even thought of that, too.

'They're going to suspect somebody, that's for sure. But it isn't going to be me. Come here, Rat, I have a little job for you to do.'

They left the roof and entered the magnificent hall of the Winter Palace. The walls were lined with goodies and twelve black puddings hung from the splendid ceiling. Uncle Charlie Weasel presented Rat with a piece of furniture.

'That table used to belong to Hog. Now this is very important, Rat. You are to take this table and put it in Foxy's old den.'

'What for, Charlie?'

'Have you ever tasted streetmouse-pie?'

'Never.'

'Neither have I. Do this for me, Rat, and I can guarantee that a piece of mouse-pie shall be yours. As for me – I am off to a meeting on Crack Willow Hill!'

Harvey and Wilhemina scampered down Foxy's Lane and stopped outside Foxy's old den. They could hardly see the door behind a tangle of ivy and robin-run-the-hedge. Foxy had not lived here for some time.

Henry Streetmouse and his friends were delighted to see them.

'We're going to a meeting at Crack Willow,' said Wilhemina. 'Our papa is in charge of it and he's all dressed up.'

'There's a robber in the forest,' said Harvey, 'he's taking everybody's food and that's what the meeting is about. You should come, Henry.'

'Too busy, mate. Look.'

Coils of rope lay all over the floor, and a pile of extra-long mouse-poles rested against a table. The table looked rather like a piece of Hog's furniture, but Wilhemina knew that it couldn't be.

'We're going to get our house back,' said Mac.

'That pussy weasel's in for a surprise, all right,' said Roscoff.

'Our house has a secret,' said the Short Mouse, who gave Wilhemina such a crafty wink that she was dying to ask what the secret was.

But the Young Stoats didn't have time — when they arrived at the crack willow tree they found its trunk already crowded with forest folk. Mrs Stoat sat between Buck Rabbit's family on one side and Hog on the other. Among the branches at the bushy end of the tree, dozens of squirrels chatted incessantly and waited for the business to begin. Foxy stooped to speak with Mole and a passing otter flopped down to observe the fuss. Uncle Charlie Weasel, who had been one of the first to arrive, was curious about the otter. He'd never tasted otter.

In the large hollow that had once been filled by the roots of the stricken willow, Mr Stoat pulled nervously at his throat and wondered whether he ought to get the meeting started. This was probably the grandest meeting ever seen on Crack Willow Hill.

He frowned and cleared his throat.

'Ahem. It gives me great pleasure to say Hello to everyone. This is a very fine turnout — really very good.'

'Get on with it, Stoaty,' boomed Badger.

'Yes. Well, as you all know, food has been disappearing. Rather a lot of it, actually. In fact I can safely say that food has been

disappearing on a grand scale and there has never been anything like it. Why, my good friend Badger has lost some black puddings . . .'

'Twelve,' bellowed Badger, 'twelve black puddings.'

'Exactly so. And this must be stopped. Who will be burgled next? *That* is the question we must ask ourselves. I declare this meeting well and truly open.'

When Mr Stoat sat down there was silence in the company; except for the squirrels, of course, who didn't know how to shut up.

'I think Papa is wonderful,' Wilhemina whispered to Harvey, who nodded to show that he agreed with her absolutely.

Then Uncle Charlie Weasel walked forward to speak. He tilted up his face so that they could hear him in the trees.

'This is a shame and a disgrace, you know,' he said loudly. 'All that food – that lovely, lovely food. All gone. And with winter coming in! Boy, I'd like to get my teeth into whoever is doing this.'

'Me too!' roared Badger. Hog muttered 'Hear, hear,' rather sadly.

'We all know,' continued Uncle Charlie

Weasel, 'that this has never happened before. Well, the first question is obvious. Are there any newcomers to the district?'

A pause occurred, some thinking was done.

'Only those mice,' said Buck Rabbit.

'Aha!' said Uncle Charlie Weasel. 'And they are from the city, don't forget. Twenty-seven of them. If you ask me, they're a pretty rough lot.'

Quite a few heads began to nod, as if aware that twenty-seven mice would require a lot of food.

Wilhemina was outraged. 'He's trying to blame our Henry Streetmouse!' she whispered fiercely to Harvey.

Badger called out, 'It's certainly possible, Stoaty. What do you think?'

'I cannot believe it,' said Mr Stoat. 'Their behaviour has always been honourable.'

'My dear nephew,' said Uncle Charlie Weasel, 'you are a soft big silly-billy. Always have been. Look at the facts of this case. Food has never gone missing before. Now, twenty-seven greedy little mousy-wousics arrive in from outside and suddenly nobody has any food left.'

'It must be them,' some squirrels shouted

from the high branches. Harvey turned right round to speak to them.

'You shut up!'

'But look here,' said Mr Stoat, facing his Uncle, 'how could such little chaps remove such large quantities of food?'

'Easy. By mouse chain.'

'Mouse chain? What's that?'

'They form a long line and pass the food along it, piece by piece, and then they hide it. Simple.'

Slowly, Badger lumbered to his feet. He had a mental picture of twelve black puddings, one after another, bobbing along a line of mice.

'By Jove,' he said, 'the clever little devils!'

Gravely, Mr Stoat nodded his head. 'Very well, Uncle, I have one last question for you. Where, if at all, did they hide all this food?'

'Why don't we look in Foxy's old den,' Uncle Charlie Weasel suggested pleasantly. 'That would seem to be a good place to start. After you, Nephew – the rest of us shall follow.'

12
Uncle Charlie Weasel Takes a Prisoner

Outside Foxy's old den a lot of huffing and puffing was going on. Twenty-seven hot and sweaty mice were doing their daily exercises. After some skipping, some press-ups and some running-on-the-spot, many of them were desperately gasping for breath.

At last Henry Streetmouse called a halt.

'Right, that'll do for now. We'll knock off for five minutes and start again.'

'Ah come on, Man, wise up,' said Mac.

'Not *again*!' said Roscoff.

'Yes, again. If we're going to show that pussy-weasel who's boss we have to be fit, we have to be strong, we have to be . . .'

We have to be supermice, he was going to say, but Harvey and Wilhemina Stoat appeared at the end of Foxy's Lane, and they were running.

'Henry, Henry, Henry!'

'You have to run, you have to hide, Uncle Charlie Weasel's coming.'

'And he says you're the robbers,' shouted Harvey. 'You have to hurry up and be quick!'

Streetmice were always ready for an emergency. There was a holly tree close by. The hairy stem of an ivy creeper ran up its trunk like a winding staircase: twenty-seven mice zoomed up and hid in the glossy foliage just as Mr Stoat, Badger and the others came into view.

They stood in a semi-circle round the door of Foxy's den, at which point Uncle Charlie Weasel took control.

'Stand back there, give me room.' Pausing only to roll up his sleeves, he let out a terrifying cry of 'CHAAAARGE!' and ran at the door, bashed it flat with his shoulder and disappeared inside while calling out at the top of his voice, 'Out, out, out, you bunch of mousy-wousies – your time is up!'

Within moments he re-appeared, carrying something.

'No food in there,' he said, 'but I found this piece of furniture. Does it belong to anyone?'

Hog raced forward. 'That's my table. Those mice had my kitchen table! Well,

that settles it, Stoaty, they *must* be the guilty ones!' And he bristled so much that his spikes seemed about to fall off.

But where were the mice? No one thought of looking up. Then Badger, who was standing under the holly tree, felt something fall on his shoulder. He picked it off, and saw that it was a very small boot.

A mouse boot. Now, he looked up.

'By Jove,' he said, 'I do believe I've found the blighters.' So saying, he gripped the tree by a low branch, gave it a good shake – and a shower of mice came tumbling down.

Those mice were running as soon as they landed. Some skipped over Foxy's tail, some darted between Mr Stoat's legs, and at least one disappeared down one of Mole's more recent holes. Within seconds there wasn't a mouse to be seen – except for one. The unfortunate Roscoff landed right in Mrs Stoat's bonnet. Harvey and Wilhemina were horrified to see Uncle Charlie Weasel grab the bonnet, mouse and all.

'Got you! Come with me, little mousy-wousy, Uncle Charlie Weasel knows what's good for you.' Then he bolted down Foxy's Lane with Roscoff firmly in his fist.

'Hey, where's he going?' yelled Badger.

'What about my black puddings? What's happening here, Stoaty?'

Mr Stoat was bewildered. He did not know where his Uncle was going, he knew nothing about Badger's black puddings and he had no idea at all what was happening.

Uncle Charlie Weasel knew exactly what was happening. He burst into his Winter Palace and found Rat where he had been posted on guard.

'Look what I got! I just grabbed him. Quick thinking, Rat, it's the only way. Oh boy, twenty-seven mousy-wousies baked in a pie!'

'But, Charlie,' Rat pointed to Roscoff as Uncle Charlie Weasel tied him up, 'you've only got one mouse.'

'Rat, Rat, you have no imagination you are so *limited*. They'll try to rescue this one, won't they. I'll get 'em all, every last one!'

And he broke joyfully into song on the spot:

'Ooooo . . . I'll gobble 'em skinned,
I'll eat 'em if tinned,
But I can't tell a lie,
Nothing beats pie,
Yes! I'd rather have mousy-wouse pie!'

13
The House
That Came Alive

It wasn't easy to find twenty-six mice who had just run for their lives into the woods. Harvey and Wilhemina looked in all kinds of likely places without seeing so much as a whisker. Harvey guessed that they must have gone back to the city, but he was wrong.

'Pssst!' someone hissed at them from the holly tree. 'I'm up here. Look out, I'm coming down.'

Henry Streetmouse landed on a tuft of grass at Harvey's feet. He'd lost an ear-ring and his hat was crooked, but otherwise he looked fine.

'I caught hold of a branch at the last minute,' he explained. 'I saw everything. Man, it was some show. We'd better hurry before that pussy-weasel does something drastic to our mate Roscoff.'

'Can we help?' said Wilhemina.

'Please?' said Harvey.

'Sure. Regard yourselves as honorary mice. Here goes.'

Henry Streetmouse sounded out three sharp whistles, and his gang of Streetmice appeared like magic. Each one carried his mouse pole at the ready and many were kitted out with coils of rope. As soon as they had lined up in rows, Henry spoke to his regiment of small warriors.

'Let's go. Let's go get Roscoff. Let's go get our house back. Let's show Mr Pussy-weasel what mousy-wousies are made of!'

With a single, lusty shout of 'Hurrah!' they set off through the woods, jogging in single file. Harvey and Wilhemina, following behind, wondered how they could have the nerve to tackle a big weasel.

A cold wind blew in gusts through the spaces in the trees where the leaves used to be. These leaves, now fallen and whipped into blizzards by the wind, blocked the forest paths with rust-coloured avalanches. Henry Streetmouse and his regiment of Streetmice ploughed straight through them – nothing was stopping them now. At last their house came into view. The flat roof, littered with autumn debris, looked as though it had just been thatched.

Henry Streetmouse called 'Halt' very quietly.

'Who has the long ropes?'

The long ropes came forward.

'But Henry,' said Wilhemina anxiously, 'how are you going to do this? He's much too big and strong.'

'And mean and nasty,' said Harvey.

'So is a streetcat,' said Henry, in the manner of one who has had many fights with many streetcats.

A party of mice raced across the ground and scurried up the legs of the house to the roof. The ropes were unfurled, lowered, and fixed to the top of the broad shelf that jutted out from the main body of the mouse house. A piece of wood rose up like a lid – to reveal a long strip of black and white . . .

Well, Harvey and Wilhemina did not know what they were.

'What do those things do?' asked Wilhemina.

'Our secret weapon,' said Henry Streetmouse. 'Just listen.' And he shouted loudly: 'JUMP!'

Immediately, twenty mice and more launched themselves boldly into the air.

Inside his Winter Palace, Uncle Charlie Weasel was about to dine rather well on a fat black pudding.

'Hmmm. Yummy yum yum,' he said, his nose all-of-a twitch, 'you must taste this, Rat, it will drive your mouth wild!' And he cut off a tiny fraction from one end.

Rat nibbled at it – or at least *tried* to nibble. Nibbling was not easy with such a tiny sample.

'Delicious, Charlie!'

'I got eleven more. Eleven. Woweee!' He offered a piece to Roscoff, who was bound hand and foot to a strut close by. 'Have a munch, mousy-wousy. It might be your last.'

'That's what you think, mate,' Roscoff said bravely.

Suddenly Rat pricked up his ears. 'I heard something on the roof, Charlie.'

'Leaves, Rat, leaves. Run up there like a good fellow and brush them off.'

Before Rat could move, the noise began. It

was unearthly. These were new sounds, neither Rat nor Uncle Charlie Weasel had ever heard their like before. A thunderstorm, it seemed, had broken out within the house itself, right against their ears, but the thunder did not stop. It rained down noise — noises high and noises low, sharps and flats and pings and twangs all jumbled up together.

'Oh Charlie, look!' Rat noticed that the house itself was moving. Dozens of little hammers had suddenly started to fly.

'Oh jeepers!' shivered Rat. 'It's alive. The house is alive, Charlie.' He took off through the door — a blurred, brown streak followed by a tail.

Now, some powerful growling notes burst through the walls. Uncle Charlie Weasel, who was stiff with fright, felt them in his very bones, and above his head eleven black puddings began to sway in a ghostly way.

'Scary, isn't it?' said Roscoff.

'Shut up, mouse!' cried Uncle Charlie Weasel, who couldn't even think properly with all the noise going on around him. This is a crazy house, he thought wildly — maybe it isn't a house at all, maybe it's something else, maybe it's . . .

Uncle Charlie Weasel stood up with his mouth hanging open and with terror in his eyes, for a mad idea had just come into his head. Maybe the house was going to eat him.

'Leave me alone, you Beast!' he screamed, and made a bolt for the door, from where he tumbled head-over-heels and fell flat on his face in a patch of wet mud.

He picked himself up and raced into the forest without daring to look back in case the house was after him. Not for years, not since he was chased by a big white goose with an orange beak, had he been so scared.

He did not see Henry Streetmouse and his Streetmouse friends dancing merrily on the black and white keys of what had once been a very grand piano.

14
Another Winter in a Welly Boot

It was very unusual for Mr Stoat, Hog and Badger to sit in silence on the trunk of the crack willow tree – but that was exactly the situation. None of them felt like talking. They sat with long faces, as if trying to get to the bottom of a great and private mystery.

Up The Avenue came the Young Stoats. Wilhemina, slightly in front of Harvey, was waving something in the air.

Badger stirred himself first.

'Look, Stoaty. What has she got there? It looks like . . . by Jove, it is! She's got one of my black puddings.'

Wilhemina came closer, panting all the way.

'We found the food, all of it, everybody's!'

'It was Uncle Charlie Weasel all the time,' gasped Harvey.

'And the furniture, we found Mr Hog's furniture.'

'Uncle Charlie Weasel took everything and he hid it in the house that makes a noise.'

There had not been such excitement on Crack Willow Hill since the early spring. Badger cradled his black pudding in his arms and stroked it, while Harvey and Wilhemina told the whole story with all its shocking details. Soon everyone knew, and a large procession of forest folk set off to see the piano-in-the-woods for themselves. Many of them were astonished to see how much food there was, and some squabbling broke out when it came to deciding who owned what. However, most of them got more or less what they had lost. Hog was so happy to recover his furniture that he did a head-over-heels and ended up looking like a ball of leaves. 'I have never been so happy,' he told Mole, who arrived late as usual.

When the sharing-out was over, Mr Stoat spoke gravely to Henry Streetmouse. This was one of those occasions when he was at his very best.

'Mr Streetmouse, my friends have asked me to say a few words to you. We do not say that we were not suspicious of you, being strangers. We do not say that we have not acted badly. What we *do* say is that we are sorry. We *do* say that every door will always be open to you on Crack Willow Hill. Welcome.'

There were cries of 'Well said, Stoaty.'

Henry Streetmouse pointed to Harvey and Wilhemina. 'We had a bit of help, you know, mate. If it hadn't been for those two we'd have been a bunch of losers. Okay, lads – three cheers for the Young Stoats.'

The cheers duly came, and Mr Stoat looked proud enough to burst.

Somewhere near the edge of the wood, not too far from the trash cans, Uncle Charlie Weasel was preparing for a long winter. Already he had gathered up armfuls of bracken and leaves and patted them into a firm, round pile. Under this manufactured mound was a welly boot.

The sky was clear above, some early stars were twinkling. A frost had turned everything crisp. Boy, it's hard to keep a welly boot warm, thought Uncle Charlie Weasel as he wiped a drip from his nose.

He stuffed some straw into his socks and

down his trousers. Strands of straw escaped from under his cap so that he looked for all the world like some scarecrow escaped from a farmer's field.

He crawled into the welly boot, scowling. There was just about room for him round the corner of the boot, though his tail was a bit squashed against two jars of crab-apple wine.

Blasted tail! he thought.

Uncle Charlie Weasel shivered once, shivered twice, and closed his weary eyes.